KT-394-250

Hattie wanted to dance.

She tried ballet.

No-one could lift her.

9

She tried ballroom.

No-one would dance with her.

She tried tap…

15

...then jive.

"I'll never be a dancer,"
Hattie thought.

She tried one more class.

She wobbled.

She wiggled.

She waggled.

Hattie was belly-dancing.

29

She was the best in class!

Did you enjoy this book?

Look out for more *Robins* titles –
first stories in only 50 words